Monsters vs. Aliens: Top Secret
Monsters vs. Aliens ™ & © 2009 DreamWorks Animation, L.L.C.

www.harpercollinschildrens.com
Library of Congress catalog card number: 2008940111
ISBN 978-0-06-156725-4
Book design by John Sazaklis
❖
First Edition

chapter one

In a distant galaxy, a planet exploded. Glowing meteors from the blast hurtled throughout the cosmos. One meteor zoomed toward Earth—specifically, toward the suburban town of Modesto, California.

There, Susan Murphy, a pretty brunette, tried to remain calm in the moments before her wedding ceremony. She had sneaked away from the frantic preparations to a gazebo in the church's garden, where she could enjoy a few minutes of peace and quiet.

"Wow, you look beautiful," a familiar voice called out.

Susan spun around. Her fiancé, Derek, was striding toward her across the lawn, looking dapper in his tuxedo.

"So do you," she replied. "I mean . . . you look handsome."

Derek stepped up into the gazebo.

"I can't wait for our honeymoon in Paris," Susan said, taking his hands. "Eating cheese and baguettes by the River Seine . . ." Her words trailed off as Derek lowered his head. "Is something wrong?"

"No!" Derek answered. "Well . . . there's been a slight change of plans. We're going . . . somewhere better. We're going to Fresno!"

Susan blinked several times. "In what universe is Fresno better than Paris?"

"In the 'I've got an audition to become Channel 23's evening news anchor' universe!" Derek replied. "The general manager wants me to come in immediately. Isn't that great?"

Biting her lip, Susan peered at her excited fiancé's face. "That's . . . amazing," she said, trying to sound enthusiastic. "As long as we're together, Fresno is the most romantic city in the whole world. I'm so proud of you."

Derek kissed her hand. "Of *us*," he corrected her. "We're a team now."

With a nod and a smile, Susan pushed him away gently. "Now get out of here," she said. "It's bad luck to see me in my dress."

"You know I don't believe that," Derek said, but he left the gazebo and hurried toward the chapel. "I'll be waiting at the altar!" he called back. "I'll be the handsome news anchor in the tux! Love ya!"

Susan waved. "I love you, too!" she replied, but as soon as Derek was inside, Susan let her hand drop. She breathed heavily, trying to let go of her disappointment about losing the Paris honeymoon of her dreams. She had never left California and always wondered about the big world beyond it.

Her thoughts were interrupted by a flash in the sky. A blazing object zoomed down out of the blue. Susan's eyes widened.

It was a meteor—rocketing directly toward her!

Susan jumped out of the gazebo and took off across the lawn, but it was difficult to run in her bridal gown and high heels.

The meteor slammed into the ground. The blast knocked Susan off her feet! An eerie green light glowed from the meteor, and then faded.

Susan's mother, Wendy, hurried out of the chapel. "Susan!" she shouted. "We're about to start!"

Dazed, Susan pulled herself upright and tottered over to her mother.

"There you are!" Wendy yelled, grabbing Susan by her arm and pulling her toward the church.

"I think . . . I just got hit by a meteorite," Susan muttered.

"Oh, Susan," her mother replied, "every bride feels that way on her wedding day."

chapter two

The wedding march played as Susan wobbled down the aisle of the chapel. Through her veil, she saw the crowded pews with everyone smiling at her. Up the aisle at the altar, Derek waited, grinning, next to the minister. On either side of Susan, her mother and father supported her by her arms.

When Susan reached the altar, Derek tenderly lifted her veil . . . and gasped in shock at the pulsing, greenish aura around her face. "Wow," he breathed, "you're glowing."

"Thank you," Susan replied groggily.

"No," Derek said. "You're *really* glowing. You're *green.*"

Derek took out the ring and started to bring it close to Susan's finger, but he couldn't even fit it over the tip.

Susan's hand was swelling, growing larger every second.

Derek glanced up. Susan was now towering over him, getting taller as he watched. She shot up toward the ceiling of the chapel until her back pressed against the roof beams.

The wedding guests gasped in astonishment as Susan continued to grow.

"You're all shrinking!" Susan cried.

"Uh-uh!" Derek called back. "You're growing!"

Susan bent over to avoid crashing through the ceiling. "Make it stop!"

The minister pulled out his cell phone from beneath his robes and dialed 911. "Get me the government!" he exclaimed. Then, to avoid being crushed by Susan's enormous foot, he dove through the open chapel window.

"This can't be happening!" Susan shouted as her hair turned white. The stretchy garter around her thigh suddenly snapped and whizzed over the heads of the crowd.

Everyone in the pews started screaming and panicking, rushing for the exits as Susan expanded even more. "It's okay!" she yelled to her guests. "We'll figure this out!"

But she continued growing, and her head smashed through the roof, popping up into the steeple. Her arms burst through the stained-glass windows on each of the church's side walls.

Painfully cramped in the chapel, Susan stood up to

her full height—now nearly fifty feet tall! The bell tower toppled to the ground, and the church splintered around her.

"Here comes the bride!" a male guest screamed in horror.

That's when a group of military helicopters swooped over the church and landed, and soldiers burst into the chapel parking lot. They had tracked the meteor as it fell through the atmosphere, and they quickly surrounded Susan.

"Make them stop!" Wendy shrieked. "It's her wedding day!"

The soldiers grabbed Susan's parents and dragged them away.

Ignoring the military, Susan poked through the wreckage of the church, searching for Derek. She pulled up a section of smashed roof and found him under the debris, dazed.

"Beam . . . hurt . . . Derek," he groaned.

Susan scooped Derek into her hand and raised him to her huge face. "Thank goodness you're okay," she bellowed. "What's happening to me?"

The soldiers below tossed up grappling hooks, which snagged onto Susan's arms.

"Don't panic," Derek moaned. "And whatever you do, don't drop me. . . ."

The grappling hook ropes grew taut as the soldiers yanked Susan's arms. Derek dropped.

Susan screamed, but Derek landed safely in a parachute net held by several Marines. They slid him off the net and hustled him away from Susan.

"Get your hands off me!" Derek shouted. "Don't you know who I am?"

Pulling back on the ropes that held her, Susan tried to follow Derek. But the soldiers tossed more grappling hooks into her hair, holding her in place. "Ow!" Susan yelled. "Please, just leave me alone!"

Then a group of Marines rushed out of a big van,

hauling a giant syringe. "Hypodermic team, now!" their captain ordered. "Go!"

The Marines jammed the gigantic needle into Susan's leg and injected her with gallons of sedative.

"No!" Susan gasped. She swatted the Marines away with her gargantuan hand, pulled the needle out of her leg, and tossed the syringe to the side.

The needle landed point first in the foot of a soldier. "Ow!" he yelled, and he passed out.

The sedative finally took effect on Susan, too. Her vast eyelids fluttered, and she crumpled to the lawn, shaking the ground like an earthquake.

Marines swarmed around her, tying her down.

"Derek . . . ," Susan moaned.

Then everything went black.

chapter three

Susan woke the next morning to a buzzing sound. She yawned and stretched. "Baby, why did you set the alarm?" she groaned. "We're on our honeymoon." Then she rolled over... and fell out of bed.

Sitting up, Susan realized that she wasn't on her honeymoon in Paris... or in Fresno. She was in a prison cell with bare metal walls.

"What's going on?" she cried.

The bed folded into the wall, and metal doors slammed shut in her cell. Susan screamed as the whole cell dropped without warning, like an elevator with its cables cut. She backed up against the wall as the cell continued to fall, the floors outside flashing by as she whizzed downward.

Then the cell stopped abruptly. Susan let out an "Oof!" as her stomach lurched.

The door slid open into a huge room with a metal table in the center. The back wall of Susan's cell pushed forward, forcing her to scurry into the bright room.

As Susan stepped toward the table slowly, she heard faint whispering. "Hello? Could you please tell me where I am?" she asked.

In the high ceiling, a panel slid open. A tube lowered into the room, spewing gallons of goopy oatmeal onto the table. A huge spoon dropped onto the pile. The ceiling panel closed.

Susan grimaced at the gross heap of oatmeal. Then she spotted movement behind her and whirled around.

A cockroach with a human body wearing a little white lab coat peered at her, letting out little clicks as it shifted in place.

"Ew!" Susan squealed. She grabbed the spoon and swatted the roach.

The cockroach ducked the spoon, and dodged as Susan swung again. He waved his human hands at her. "Careful!" he cried. "Easy now!"

Susan paused, holding the spoon ready to strike.

"Please," the cockroach said, dusting himself off. "This magnificent brain of mine will be in a museum one day, so let's not squash it, all right?"

Gaping at the cockroach, Susan dropped the spoon and stepped backward, slipping on something sticky.

Susan looked down to discover that she'd crushed what looked like a large, blue booger. She picked it up and studied it.

An eye appeared on the blob, studying her right back. Then a mouth joined the eye. "Hi, there!"

Grossed out, Susan flicked the blue goo off her hand.

"Forgive him," the cockroach said. "He has no brain."

"Turns out you don't need one," the goo added.

Susan stiffened—something was crawling on her head. She peered up and met the eyes of a bizarre creature that looked like a combination of an ape and a fish.

"Legally, I've got to warn you," the fish-ape said. "I kind of remember karate." He laughed as he slid down the long length of Susan's giant body. He landed on the ground and smiled up at Susan, who gaped in shock.

"She's speechless," the fish-ape said.

"She?" the blue thing asked.

"Yes, B.O.B.," the roach replied. "We are in the presence of the rare female monster. Gentlemen, we are not making a very good first impression." He nodded up at Susan. "I am Dr. Cockroach, Ph.D." He pointed at the fish-ape. "That's The Missing Link. You've already met Benzoate Ostelyzene Bicarbonate over there, better known as B.O.B. Might we ask your name, madam?"

"Susan," Susan answered.

"No," B.O.B. said. "We mean your *monster* name. What do people scream when they see you coming? Like, 'Look out! Here comes . . .'"

"Susan," Susan finished.

"Susan!" B.O.B. screamed. "Oh, that is scary."

Susan stared at the monsters. "Tell me this isn't real," she muttered. "I had a nervous breakdown at the wedding. . . ."

Backing away slowly, Susan bumped into a fuzzy wall. She looked up into the bug-eyed face of a 350-foot-tall insect. The gargantuan bug screeched, and Susan screamed, bolting across the room.

"Don't scare Insectosaurus!" The Missing Link yelled. He rubbed the giant insect and cooed, "Who's a handsome bug?"

Susan ran her hands over the wall, panicking. "Every room has a door!" she cried. "Please—I don't belong here! Let me out!" She started pounding on the wall, which shook from the impact of her giant fists.

A huge door near Susan slid open, and a military general buzzed in on a jet pack. "Monsters!" he ordered. "Get back in your cells!"

Dr. Cockroach and The Missing Link hurried back into their cells, but B.O.B. stopped to absorb all the oatmeal before he left the room. Bright lights flashed in front of Insectosaurus, hypnotizing him and leading him into his cell.

The general hovered in front of Susan. "My name is General W. R. Monger," he told her. "I'm in charge of this facility. Now, follow me."

chapter four

usan stepped onto a vast conveyor belt that lurched sideways through the cavernous monster prison. The general buzzed about her with his jet pack on. They passed a busy control center in which military personnel sat, staring at Susan as she went by.

"In 1950, it was decided that the public could not handle the truth about monsters," General Monger explained. "So the government convinced the world that monsters were the stuff of legend and then locked them away in this facility."

"But I'm not a monster," Susan protested. "I'm not a danger to anyone—"

"Madam," the general interrupted, "you are five stories tall and weigh 23,632 pounds and eight ounces.

Now, let's say you decided you didn't like Florida—"

"No!" Susan broke in. "I love Florida! My Nana lives there!"

"You say that now," General Monger replied, "but eventually, you'll turn on Florida. They always do."

The transporter lurched as it rode upward along a curving track. "How long will I be here?" Susan asked.

"Indefinitely," the general answered.

"Can I contact my parents? Or Derek? Do they know where I am?"

General Monger shook his head. "Negative. And they never will. This place is wrapped in a cover-up and deep-fried in a conspiracy. You will have zero contact with the outside world."

Susan crossed her arms. "This isn't fair," she argued. "I haven't done anything wrong. There was this meteorite—"

"Yes," the general interrupted again, "we know. You absorbed whatever was inside it."

"So if you know what turned me into a giant," Susan said, "you can fix me."

The general pointed at his chest. "See these medals?" he asked. "Not one of them is for helping a monster."

The transporter changed direction again, plummeting downward. It stopped next to Susan's cell.

"We redecorated," General Monger said, "to keep you all calmlike."

Susan peered inside. The cell looked almost the same, except now a tiny, human-sized poster of a kitten hanging from a tree covered one metal wall. The caption read HANG IN THERE!

"But I don't want a poster," Susan sobbed. "I want a real kitten in a real tree. I want to go home."

"Don't think of this as a prison," the general said. "Think of it as a hotel you never leave because it's locked from the outside."

The transporter pushed Susan into her cell, and she tumbled to the floor, slumping against the wall.

"Oh, one other thing," General Monger said. "The government has changed your name to . . . Ginormica." The cell doors slid shut.

Alone in her cell, Susan hugged her knees, feeling more miserable than she'd ever felt in her life.

chapter five

Over the next three weeks, Susan became more comfortable with her fellow monsters. She even agreed to let Dr. Cockroach perform experiments to see if he could shrink her.

The intelligent roach built a machine out of scavenged parts and hooked it up to Susan's head with wires. He laughed like a mad scientist as he attached a radio antenna to his contraption.

"Doctor," Susan said, "I'd prefer if you didn't do your laugh."

The Missing Link and B.O.B. gathered around to watch. "I can't believe you're still letting him experiment on you," The Missing Link said.

"What choice do I have?" Susan replied. "If he can make me normal—or even six foot eight—I can get back to Derek. Throw the switch, Doctor. But don't do the laugh."

"Yes, the switch!" the cockroach cried. He let out his evil cackle again but broke it off. "Sorry, I can't help myself." He switched on his machine.

Bolts of energy sizzled around Susan and arced back into the machine, which exploded in a shower of sparks. Susan screamed and passed out.

She woke with the monsters looking down at her. "Am I small again?"

"I'm afraid not, my dear," Dr. Cockroach replied. "In fact, you may have grown."

The monsters were standing on her face. They climbed off, and Susan sat up, peeling electrodes from her body. "That's okay, Doc," she said. "We'll try again tomorrow."

The Missing Link shook his head. "You really don't get it, do you? No monster has ever gotten out of here."

"That's not true," B.O.B. argued. "The Invisible Man did."

The Missing Link grimaced. "No, he didn't," he said. "We just told you that."

"He died of a heart attack twenty-five years ago," added Dr. Cockroach.

"In that very chair," The Missing Link said, pointing across the room. "He's still there."

B.O.B. stared at the seemingly empty chair, horrified.

"You see?" The Missing Link asked Susan. "Nobody's ever getting out of here—"

The door slid open and General Monger zoomed inside. "Good news, monsters!" the general announced. "You're getting out!"

"—until today," The Missing Link finished.

General Monger led the monsters onto the transporter, which took them through the top-security prison. On the way, he explained that Earth was under attack by an alien robot, and there was nothing the world's armies could do to stop it. So they were calling in the monsters.

"So let me get this straight," The Missing Link said. "You want us to fight an alien robot?"

General Monger nodded. "In exchange for saving Earth, the president of the United States will grant you your freedom."

Susan gasped, and the other monsters' eyes grew wide. There was nothing they wanted more than freedom.

As the transporter entered an airplane hangar, Susan said, "I can't believe it—soon I'll be back in Derek's arms." She glanced at her enormous limbs. "Or he'll be in mine."

The Missing Link sighed happily. "I'll be eating fresh frogs back in the old lagoon."

"And I'll return to my lab and finish my experiments," B.O.B. added.

Dr. Cockroach shook his head. "No, that's me, B.O.B."

"Then I'll be a giant lady," B.O.B. said.

"That's Susan, B.O.B.," Dr. Cockroach corrected.

"Fine," B.O.B. said, contracting into a small ball. "Then I'll go to Modesto and be with Derek."

"That's still Susan, B.O.B.," said The Missing Link.

They arrived at a massive transport plane and climbed

aboard. The plane soon took off, followed by a helicopter. Its big, bright lights hypnotized Insectosaurus, who came plodding after them on the ground.

Susan stared out the window as they flew over San Francisco. The city had been evacuated, and the last cars and trucks were being led across the Golden Gate Bridge by the military. The plane landed on the highway, and the monsters stepped out into the sunshine. That's when they saw the enormous robot they had to fight.

"Wait!" Susan called to General Monger as he boarded the plane. "You didn't say anything about it being huge!"

The plane took off, leaving the monsters with the massive robot, which shone a beam from its eye on them.

"Hello!" B.O.B. shouted. "How are you doing? We are here to destroy you." The robot lurched toward Susan, crushing B.O.B. with an enormous foot.

Susan ran toward the city in terror.

"I got him, you guys!" B.O.B. yelled from under the robot's foot. "Please tell me he's slowing down!"

But the alien machine wasn't slowing down. It relentlessly followed Susan through the city streets. Then she realized that her feet were the same size as the abandoned cars around her. Susan jammed each foot down on a car and roller-skated quickly toward the bridge. "Okay, I got this," she muttered.

But when Susan reached the traffic still trying to escape across the bridge, she found she couldn't stop. "Excuse me!" she shouted to the military. "Coming through! No control!" She whizzed right past the army checkpoint and onto the bridge.

When the driver of an oil tanker saw Susan, he hit his brakes, causing the truck to flip over and crush a car beneath it. Susan ran toward the tanker to help the passengers in the flattened car.

But before Susan could help, the robot reached her and began grabbing at her with its claws. Susan ducked, and the robot missed her, hitting the bridge instead. The whole bridge wobbled. People screamed in their cars.

The robot attacked Susan again, snapping bridge cables with its claws as it tried to catch her. When it got close enough to her, a giant panel in its midsection opened. Inside the robot was grinding equipment that worked like a trash compactor.

Susan backed up against the other side of the bridge, but another cable snapped, and she tumbled toward the robot's grinders. Pieces of the bridge were ground to dust by the robot's innards. Susan screamed.

Above the bridge, the helicopter guiding Insectosaurus turned off its hypnotizing lights. The colossal insect screeched at the robot, then shot a wad of silk goo into the robot's eye.

The robot was blinded long enough for Susan to crawl away.

Insectosaurus hurried to the edge of the crumpled bridge and pulled on it, flattening it out again.

Meanwhile, B.O.B., The Missing Link, and Dr. Cockroach caught up to Susan and the robot.

"The robot's trying to kill me!" Susan called. "Why is it doing that—?"

She was interrupted by one of the robot's claws closing around her body.

The Missing Link, B.O.B., and Dr. Cockroach gasped in horror.

chapter six

The robot's claw wriggled . . . and slowly opened. Susan had pushed the robot's metal pincers apart, using only her brute strength.

"Wow!" The Missing Link breathed.

Susan stopped, as amazed by her power as the monsters were. Then the robot shoved her to the pavement, bashing a hole in the bridge. Susan clung to a girder as abandoned cars toppled into the water below.

People still in their cars shrieked as their vehicles rolled toward the hole. Susan stuck out her leg just in time and blocked them from falling.

"You're doing great!" B.O.B. cheered.

"I'm doing *everything*!" replied Susan.

The Missing Link jumped atop a smashed car. "Not for long! Come on, guys—let's take this thing down!" He charged at the robot.

But the robot had a shield that shocked The Missing Link, sending him flying backward. He smacked into the hood of a car, squashing it. The Missing Link was out cold.

"A deflector shield," Dr. Cockroach muttered. "Typical." He scurried up Susan's leg until he was as high as the robot's grinding hatch. Dr. Cockroach let out his evil laugh. "You can't crush a cockroach!" he cried, and jumped into the hatch.

"Ow! That hurts!" Dr. Cockroach screamed as the grinders roughed him up. He pushed past the grinding equipment and into the robot, where he found a tangle of wires. "Here we go," the roach said, and he grabbed two wires and jammed them together.

A violent electrical explosion knocked Dr. Cockroach out of the back of the robot. He landed next to The Missing Link, and now both of them were unconscious.

Outside, just as Insectosaurus was reaching for the robot, the wires that Dr. Cockroach had crossed caused the robot's single eye to light up. The eye blazed at Insectosaurus, hypnotizing him. He froze.

"B.O.B.!" Susan screamed. "Help me—we have to get these people off the bridge!"

"Got it!" B.O.B. replied. He picked up a car filled with screaming passengers and started to toss it over the edge.

"No, B.O.B.!" Susan scolded. "Move the median dividers out of the way!"

B.O.B. put the car down. "My bad," he said. He slunk over to the dividers and began to eat them. Soon he'd made enough space for the trapped cars to escape.

Susan grabbed on to the robot and struggled with it, holding it back until the final occupied car was safely off the bridge.

She couldn't hold the robot forever—it was too strong. "Link!" she called. But The Missing Link was still knocked out. "B.O.B.!" she hollered.

"Ugh," B.O.B. replied, looking greenish from eating the medians. "I don't feel so good."

Susan braced herself against the flailing robot and took a deep breath. "Okay," she told herself. "You can do this."

Letting go of the robot, Susan reached out to grab bundles of bridge cables in both hands. With a flick of her wrists, she looped the cables around the robot's arms and yanked as hard as she could.

The robot tipped over, crashing down onto the bridge.

Susan leaped out of the way, grabbing Dr. Cockroach and The Missing Link as she rolled to safety off the bridge's crumbling span.

The robot toppled into the water and then tumbled against the shore. An enormous chunk of bridge sliced down behind the robot, hitting it squarely on its slotted neck.

The robot's head popped off.

Next to Susan on the twisted roadway, The Missing Link stirred. Finally awake, he stared at the collapsed bridge and the smashed robot below.

"What happened?" he asked. "What did I miss?

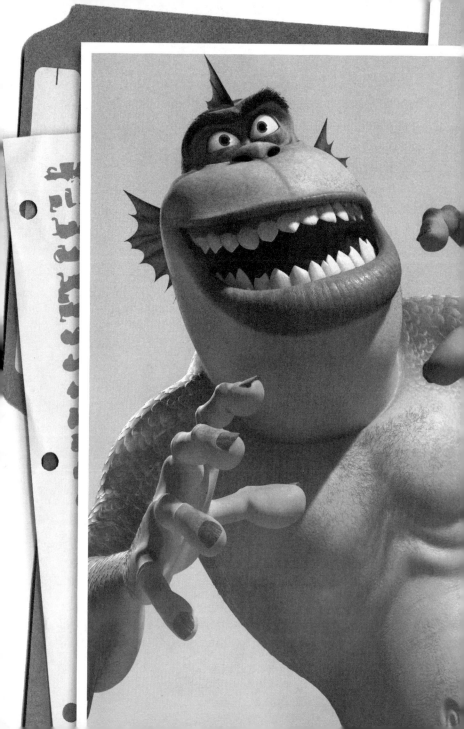

chapter seven

In the transport plane, the monsters recovered from their battle. Susan paced, too amped up to sit. "Three weeks ago, if you'd asked me to defeat a giant alien robot, I would've said, 'No can do.' But I did it! Did you see how strong I was?"

"You were heroic, my dear," Dr. Cockroach said. "I loved how you saved all those people. Nice touch."

"Thanks," Susan replied. "Now I can't wait to get back to my normal life."

The other monsters stared at her. "Uh . . . ," The Missing Link said finally, "so tell me exactly how that works. You know, with you being a giant and all."

"I'm not going to be a giant forever," Susan answered. "Derek won't rest until we've found a cure. We're a team."

B.O.B. closed his eye. "I love Derek," he breathed. "I'd like to meet him."

"I would, as well," Dr. Cockroach added. "Dereks are few and far between."

"Really?" Susan asked, surprised. "You guys want to meet Derek?"

The Missing Link crossed his arms. "I knew it," he groused. "She's ashamed of us."

"No!" Susan protested. "You guys are heroes. You just saved San Francisco. More importantly, you're my friends. Come meet Derek and my family."

General Monger drifted into the cargo hold from the cockpit. "First stop, Modesto," he announced. He jetted up to Susan's eye level. "Ginormica, I let your family know you're coming. I also called the Modesto police and told them not to shoot at you."

"Thanks, General," said Susan.

Within the hour, Susan, The Missing Link, B.O.B., and Dr. Cockroach stood in front of Susan's parents' house. "Okay, remember," Susan warned her friends nervously, "these people aren't used to seeing . . . um . . . anything like . . . you. So just be . . . you know, cool. Follow my lead."

Just then Susan accidentally stepped on her parents' fence, crushing it. The monsters instantly started smashing what was left of the fence, growling and roaring. The Missing Link tore a mailbox out of the ground and hurled it into the windshield of a parked car.

"Stop!" Susan exclaimed. "That was an accident! Don't destroy anything!"

"Would you make up your mind?" The Missing Link asked, annoyed.

The front door opened and Wendy bustled out. "Susan?" she called. She was followed outside by Susan's father and her friends.

"Mom! Daddy!" Susan shouted.

Her mother and father rushed down the walk, and each of them hugged one of Susan's enormous ankles. Susan's friends hurried after them.

"Did they experiment on you?" Wendy asked.

"No, Mom," Susan replied. "I'm fine." She breathed a sigh of relief. But then she noticed the frightened, frozen smiles around her. Susan gestured at the monsters. "It's okay, they're with me. These are my new friends."

Dr. Cockroach bowed. *"Enchanté,"* he greeted everyone in French.

B.O.B. engulfed Wendy in a sticky hug. She tried to scream, but his goo muffled her voice. "Oh, Derek," B.O.B. gushed, "I missed you so much!"

"No, B.O.B.!" Susan shouted. "You're suffocating my mother!"

B.O.B. hastily withdrew.

Wendy gasped, shaking uncontrollably.

"Sorry, Mom," Susan said. "He's a hugger." She peered down at the group . . . and realized someone was missing. "Where's Derek?"

"He's at work, sweetie," Wendy replied gently.

"Well, we're not celebrating without him!" Susan announced, and she strode toward the road.

"Susan!" her mother shrieked. "What about your . . . *friends?*"

"Put out the chips and dip!" Susan hollered. "I'll be right back!"

Susan found Derek at the Channel 172 studio. She reached into the studio, grabbed him with her giant hand, and raised him to her face.

"Oh, Derek," she said, "you wouldn't believe the last three weeks. Thinking about you was the only thing that kept me sane."

"Can't . . . breathe!" Derek gasped from within her grip. "Ribs . . . collapsing!"

"Oh, I'm sorry!" Susan said, setting him down on the roof. "I'm still getting used to my new strength."

Derek inhaled. "You really are big."

"Yeah, but I'm still me," Susan assured him. "Together we can find a way to get me back to normal."

Derek smoothed down his tie. "Look at this from my perspective. I have an audience that depends on me. You expect me to put that on hold while you try to undo what's happened to you . . . that I had nothing to do with?"

"I thought we would face whatever happened to *either* of us together," Susan replied softly. "Isn't that what marriage is about?"

"Well . . . ," Derek said, "technically, we're not married. Um . . . I checked with a lawyer. Don't crush me for saying this, but this will never work out. It's over." He stood up on the station roof. "Good luck, Susan," Derek said, and then he opened the roof door and stepped inside.

Heartbroken, Susan stumbled away from the studio, wandering through Modesto. She finally stopped beside a gas station and sat down.

Minutes later, Dr. Cockroach, B.O.B., and The Missing Link sat down next to her.

"Wow," Dr. Cockroach said. "Your parents know how to throw a party."

"The ladies were all over me," The Missing Link added.

B.O.B. blinked his eye. "I must've been at a different party," he said, confused. "Nobody seemed to like me. I think the dessert gave me a fake phone number."

"Ah, who are we kidding?" The Missing Link groaned. "We could save every city on the planet and everyone would still treat us like . . . monsters."

"Right," Susan agreed miserably. "Monsters."

"So . . . ," The Missing Link asked, "how's Derek?"

Susan tried to swallow her sadness. "Derek's . . . awesome. He's terrific—"

"Susan, please," Dr. Cockroach interrupted. "We waded through your trail of tears to get here."

Susan glanced down the road, which had giant puddles along its length. She dropped her head into her hands. "Derek is a pompous jerk," she muttered.

B.O.B. raised his face to the sky. "NO!" he wailed.

"Yes," Susan replied. She shook her head in frustration. "There was no 'us'. There was only Derek. What was *wrong* with me? The only reason Derek cared about me was because I did whatever he wanted."

"Yeah," The Missing Link said. "When we first met you, you were kind of a . . ."

"Pushover!" Dr. Cockroach and B.O.B. finished.

Susan tightened her hands into fists. "No more being pushed around!" she decided. "By people, or robots, or *anything*! Why did I even *want* to be normal? The only cool stuff I've ever done happened *after* I became a giant! Fighting an alien robot? That was amazing!" She kneeled beside her friends. "Meeting you guys? Amazing!"

A loud screech made them all look up, and Susan

saw Insectosaurus looming on the other side of the gas station.

"Good point, Insecto," The Missing Link replied. "Don't shortchange yourself, Susan."

Susan nodded. "I'm never going to shortchange myself again. And the name is . . . Ginormica!"

"Yes!" The Missing Link cheered.

Susan blinked as a bright beam of light shone down on her.

Then she screamed as the ray whisked her up into the sky.

chapter eight

"Ginormica!" the monsters hollered.

Susan struggled, but she was hauled up by the light beam toward a creepy spaceship overhead.

Insectosaurus shot a stream of webbing, snagged Susan's foot, and tried to pull her back down.

Laser fire sizzled out of the spaceship. One of the lasers hit Insectosaurus, blasting him.

"No!" Susan shrieked. Insectosaurus looked terribly hurt.

The last thing Susan saw before she was sucked into the spaceship was Insectosaurus lying on the ground, its eyes fluttering shut.

The light beam dropped Susan into a huge, metallic chamber that looked like a deployment hangar. All around were hundreds of robots. Susan climbed to her feet, looking for a way out. She took a step, which activated an energy field around her, trapping her inside. When Susan touched the energy field, it zapped her hand painfully.

An alien zipped into the chamber on a hover board. He had an enormous purplish-blue head with four eyes, stood on a mess of gross-looking tentacles, and wore an ill-fitting uniform. "I am Gallaxhar!" the alien announced. "You must be terrified!"

"Hardly," Susan replied.

Gallaxhar looked disappointed, but then he lifted his tentacles. "To the extraction chamber!"

The energy field around Susan rose, carrying her along as it followed Gallaxhar deeper into the spaceship.

"What do you want from me?" Susan asked as they traveled a long hallway.

Gallaxhar peered back. "You absorbed the Quantonium. It's rightfully mine," he replied.

Squinting her eyes, Susan seethed.

"That's what all this is about? You destroyed San Francisco . . . you terrified millions of people . . . you killed my friend. Just to get me?!"

"Silence! Your voice is grating on my ear nubs. It's a shame you won't be around to see what the power of Quantonium can do in the tentacles of someone who knows how to use it."

"I know how to use it just fine!" Susan yelled, and she punched the energy field.

"Don't bother," Gallaxhar sneered. "That force field is impenetrable."

Susan slammed her fist into the energy field again, punching right through it, knocking Gallaxhar off his hover board.

"What the . . . ?" Gallaxhar exclaimed. He scrambled back onto his hover board and took off. Susan tore out of the force field and started to run away.

Gallaxhar ordered a metal door to slide shut between him and Susan. "Ha!" he laughed. "That should stop your puny—"

But Susan smashed right through the door. She barreled after the alien, crashing through more doors and damaging the spaceship as she chased him.

Gallaxhar zipped onto the spaceship's bridge, which had a view of Earth through its windshield and was filled with control panels and computers. One side of the room ended in a ledge high above a deep, dark chamber. Down below was a tangle of alien technology, as well as a gigantic statue of Gallaxhar. Susan caught the alien and knocked him off his hover board again. Gallaxhar tumbled over the side, plopping onto a catwalk halfway down.

Susan jumped and landed next to him. Gallaxhar scrambled toward a circular landing at the end of the catwalk, with Susan close behind. He reached the wall and pulled a lever.

A glass tube dropped over Susan, trapping her inside. She tried to smash her way out, but the glass was too thick to break.

"Computer, begin extraction!" Gallaxhar shouted.

Smoky gasses in the tube glowed with yellow light, and Susan screamed in pain as green wisps of Quantonium were pulled out of her.

Quickly shrinking, Susan kept punching the walls of the tube until she passed out.

When Susan woke up, she didn't know how much time had passed, but she could see that the giant statue of Gallaxhar now held a glowing ball of Quantonium in its outstretched tentacles. And Susan was now her original size. She was surprised by how weak she felt.

The extraction chamber lifted up, and Gallaxhar approached, smiling smugly down at Susan. "Finally I can rebuild my civilization on a new planet. Any thoughts on where I should 'set up shop'? Your planet, perhaps?" he mocked.

Susan jumped to her feet. "You can't!" she yelled. "There are innocent people down there!" She charged at him, but Gallaxhar effortlessly held her back with a single tentacle.

"There were innocent people on my home planet before it was destroyed," Gallaxhar told Susan as she slumped in defeat. "But then, I'm the one who destroyed it. Computer! Initialize cloning machine!" he ordered before continuing on. "Many zentons ago, I discovered Quantonium deep in the bowels of . . ."

Just then, the cloning machine dropped down on Gallaxhar. After a beat, it lifted with a hydraulic hiss.

". . . I was deemed a lunatic and a psychopath. . . ."

The machine stamped down on Gallaxhar yet again.

"But the word was passed that the High Senate of Maxilon would find me guilty of high treason. Me! Who had served so bravely on the moons of . . ."

The machine continued stamping down around the alien overlord, creating Gallaxhar clone after Gallaxhar clone.

"And I vowed from that day on that I would not rest until the Quantonium was mine. Let the birth of my new planet begin!"

As Susan watched in helpless horror, the Gallaxhar clones gathered in the middle of the room. A mechanical assembly line outfitted each set of clones with weapons, and the aliens headed toward the deployment hangar.

Bathed in the eerie light of the Quantonium, Susan lowered her head in misery.

chapter nine

Gallaxhar," Gallaxhar ordered, "take the prisoner to the incinerator!"

"By whose authority?" the clone demanded.

Gallaxhar puffed himself up. "By the will of Gallaxhar, of course!"

"That is correct," the clone replied, and he led Susan along a corridor deep into the spaceship.

They were taking a sharp turn when someone shouted, "Halt!"

Susan raised her head. Her eyes widened in amazement—it was The Missing Link! Standing beside him were Dr. Cockroach and B.O.B. All three were dressed in Gallaxhar uniforms. Susan wiped away her tears and smiled at The Missing Link, who winked.

"I . . . Gallaxhar, command you to hand over the prisoner this instant," The Missing Link ordered.

The clone glared. "Gallaxhar does not take orders from anyone!"

"Yeah, but . . . ," The Missing Link argued, "I am Gallaxhar."

"Clearly, you are defective beyond repair!" the clone announced. He waved his tentacles in alarm. "Guards!" he screeched. "Take this defective clone to the incinerator!"

The monsters all stared at the clone in shock, expecting guards to appear.

"What are you waiting for?" the clone prodded Dr. Cockroach and B.O.B. "You and you!"

"Seriously?" Dr. Cockroach asked.

"Yes," the clone replied. "Take the prisoner and the defective clone to the incinerator." He handed Dr. Cockroach a small card. "And here's a security pass just in case. Would you like a gun?"

"Yes, I would," B.O.B. replied. "Hey guys, look!"

"You know where the incinerator is, of course?" asked the clone, before he left. "Go all the way down this hallway. Take the elevator down to the incinerator level."

The monsters turned the corner.

"I can't believe you came to save me!" Susan breathed. "I don't know what to say."

"You don't have to say anything," said Dr. Cockroach. "After all . . ."

Just then he spotted a group of clones approaching,

and then mimicked what a clone would have said.

". . . nothing but a filthy carbon-based life-form. We should take her to the incinerator!"

"Hail, Gallaxhar," droned the clones.

"Hail, Gallaxhar," replied Dr. Cockroach. The clones continued on their way.

"All right. Time for you to go, my dear," ordered Dr. Cockroach.

"Shouldn't Ginormica be helping us?" B.O.B asked.

Susan shook her head sadly. "I wish I could," she replied. "But I'm not Ginormica anymore. Good luck to you guys!"

Nodding his head, The Missing Link handed Susan the gun. "Here, you might need this."

The monsters entered the elevator, leaving Susan feeling disappointed in herself. B.O.B. spoke. "I once read something profound," B.O.B. said. "It changed the way I look at the world. It said, 'Objects in the mirror may be larger than they appear.'" With those words, the doors closed.

Susan peered into the elevator door, staring at her reflection, replaying B.O.B.'s words in her mind. Then, abruptly, the elevator dinged. The door opened to reveal a bunch of clones. Susan ran into the enormous clone room.

She spotted the original Gallaxhar high up in the control area, shaking his fist. Across the room were B.O.B. and The Missing Link, fighting against the clones. B.O.B. had grown huge by absorbing the clones, and The Missing

Link was knocking out the remaining ones by swinging around on the Gallaxhar statue and kicking them.

Dr. Cockroach, laughing maniacally, stood on top of a bank of computers. He pulled out wires as sparks flickered everywhere.

"*Ship has sustained internal damage,*" the ship's computer announced. "*Invasion no longer possible.*"

As Susan rushed across the wide room, The Missing Link, B.O.B., and Dr. Cockroach hopped on a hover board and headed toward the exit.

"Close the blast doors!" Gallaxhar ordered the computer.

Before the monsters could reach the exit, glass blast doors slammed down in front of their hover board. They swerved before hitting it.

Then another blast door slid down, blocking Susan from her friends, who were now trapped in a small space between the two doors.

Another blast door had closed behind Susan, on the far end of the room. Only one of the clones chasing her had gotten through. She ran to the door that kept her from her friends. Reaching it, she turned around.

The clone zoomed toward her on his hover board, aiming to smash her.

Susan leaped out of the way.

The clone slammed into the glass. His hover board shattered, and the alien was knocked unconscious.

"Computer, divert Quantonium to bridge," an irritated Gallaxhar ordered. The green glow of Quantonium ran along the edge of the ship into the center and then directly up toward the bridge.

Susan pressed her hand against the door, wishing her friends could help her. But they were trapped. It was up to her. "Hang tight," she told them. "I'll get you out of here."

Suddenly, Susan had an idea. She grabbed the clone's hover board and another one floating nearby, and she rushed to Gallaxhar. He fired his laser gun, but she avoided his shots. She zoomed at him, knocking the gun out of his tentacle. The gun slid across the control room.

Gallaxhar shrieked and scrambled toward the glowing orb. Susan dove at him, grabbing his tentacles and pulling him to the floor.

Susan and Gallaxhar wrestled desperately. As the alien began to overpower her, Susan stretched her arm toward the gun . . . but it was too far away.

So she wriggled around to face the alien. She grabbed his antennae and yanked them—hard.

"Ow!" Gallaxhar screamed. "My zaznoids!" He let go of her.

Susan rolled toward the gun and snagged it, instantly aiming it at the alien. She climbed to her feet, standing under the glowing green Quantonium. "It's over, Gallaxhar."

The spaceship rocked violently, and Susan struggled to stay on her feet.

"Ship has taken heavy interior damage," the computer announced. *"Reactor core meltdown. Total annihilation in T minus two minutes."*

Susan aimed the gun at Gallaxhar again. She wasn't sure what to do—even if she killed the alien and managed to escape the exploding spaceship, her friends were trapped between the blast doors. She couldn't leave them!

Gallaxhar laughed. "I think it's time we cut ourselves a little deal, huh? I'll open the doors if you split the Quantonium with me."

Susan closed one eye and pointed the gun. Gallaxhar winced, preparing himself for death.

Raising the gun, Susan fired a laser overhead. She blasted off one of the statue's tentacles holding the orb.

Quantonium showered Susan.

The statue's sheared-off tentacle toppled onto Gallaxhar, trapping him underneath.

"Total annihilation in T minus one minute," the computer announced.

Glowing green, Susan was still growing as she raced

to the blast door that imprisoned her friends. She easily smashed it open with her giant's strength.

"It's Ginormica!" B.O.B. cheered.

Susan grabbed the monsters in one hand and used her other fist to smash her way through the spaceship's walls.

"*Total annihilation in T minus thirty seconds,*" the computer intoned.

Smashing everything in her path, Susan made hole after hole until she reached a windy ledge outside the spaceship. She gripped the edge of the hole and scanned the sky.

"*Total annihilation in T minus fifteen seconds,*" the computer announced.

"Where's General Monger?" Susan cried.

"He's supposed to be here!" The Missing Link yelled.

"*Nine seconds,*" the computer counted down. "*Eight.*"

General Monger popped up in front of the hole, riding a monstrous butterfly. Insectosaurus had transformed!

"Insectosaurus!" The Missing Link shouted happily. "You're alive!"

"Sorry I'm late," General Monger called. "Get on!"

Susan and the monsters jumped down onto Insectosaurus' back. The colossal butterfly beat its pretty wings and whooshed away from the ship.

They had just gotten far enough away when the spaceship exploded in a massive fireball—but not before an escape pod was seen shooting away from the destruction.

The cheers of the crowd on the White House lawn were deafening.

"Well, it looks as though Earth has been saved by the most unlikely of heroes," a reporter told his viewers. "Now the president will present the monsters with the Presidential Beads of Gratitude!"

Susan, The Missing Link, B.O.B., and Dr. Cockroach lined up beside the president and waved to the thunderous crowd. Up above, Butterflyosaurus and several Air Force jets buzzed past in a flyby.

In the crowd, Susan's mother and father sobbed with pride.

President Hathaway smiled at the monsters. "Job well done," he praised them, reading from a sheet of paper. "Earth has been saved, and we owe it all to you. In appreciation, we will return you to a maximum security prison of your choice."

The President noticed the monsters' horrified faces, and he peered at his paper. "Old speech," he said. "Sorry." He pulled another sheet from his pocket and read it. "In recognition, the government would like to offer you your own refuge."

The crowd cheered again, and Susan, Dr. Cockroach, B.O.B., and The Missing Link all hugged each other, beaming happily.